# My Cat Looks Like My Dad

## Thao Lam

Owlkids Books

My cat looks like my dad.

They both love milk.

And sardines. Ewwww ...

My cat loves belly rubs.

So does my dad.

My cat and my dad always start
their mornings with stretches.

And their afternoons with naps.

My cat is afraid of heights.

My dad is also
afraid of heights.

My dad is a great singer.

My cat thinks he's
a great singer.

Mom is always picking up
after my dad.

And my cat.

And neither of them ever replaces
the toilet paper roll.

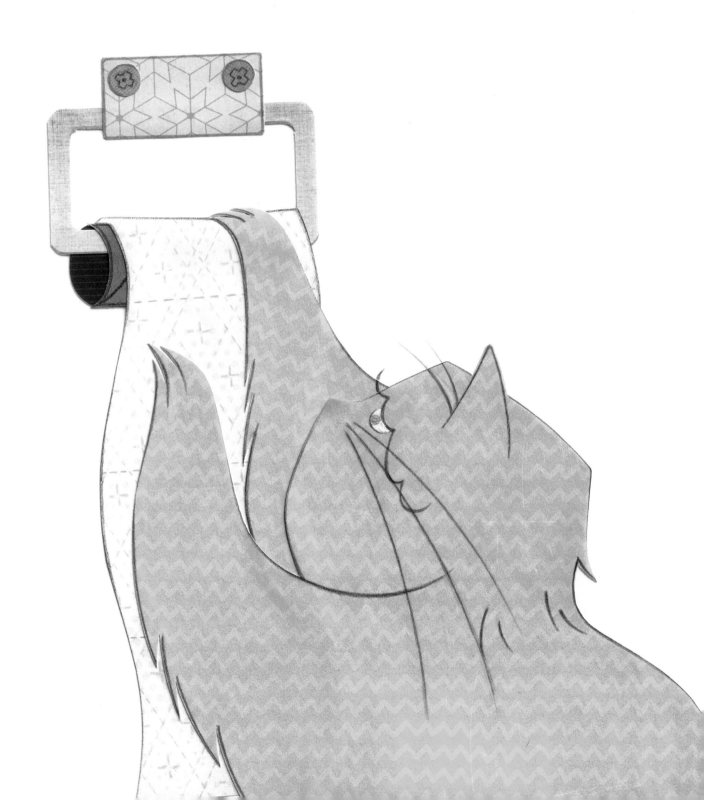

They are both brave.

Some of the time.

They both love boxes.

All of the time.

Yup, my cat looks like my dad.
And me? I look like my mom.

We both have wild hair.

Our eyes are the same color.

And we both love to dance!

Mom and Dad
always say,

Family is what you make it.

Family is what you make it.

Owlkids Books acknowledges the financial support of the Canada Council for the Arts, the Ontario Arts Council,
the Government of Canada through the Canada Book Fund (CBF), and the Government of Ontario through
the Ontario Media Development Corporation's Book Initiative for our publishing activities.

| Published in Canada by | Published in the US by |
|---|---|
| Owlkids Books Inc. | Owlkids Books Inc. |
| 1 Eglinton Avenue East | 1700 Fourth Street |
| Toronto, ON M4P 3A1 | Berkeley, CA 94710 |

Library of Congress Control Number: 2018944999

Library and Archives Canada Cataloguing in Publication

Lam, Thao, author, illustrator
My cat looks like my dad / Thao Lam.

ISBN 978-1-77147-351-4 (hardcover)
I. Title.

PS8623.A466 M9 2019          jC813'.6          C2018-903196-4

Edited by Karen Li
Designed by Alisa Baldwin

Manufactured in Shenzhen, Guangdong, China, in October 2018, by WKT Co. Ltd.
Job #18CB1092

A          B          C          D          E          F

Publisher of Chirp, Chickadee and OWL     |     Owlkids Books is a division of     Bayard CANADA
www.owlkidsbooks.com

To Logan and Titus, thank you for
the opening line. And to Maddie for
teaching me the last one—T.L.